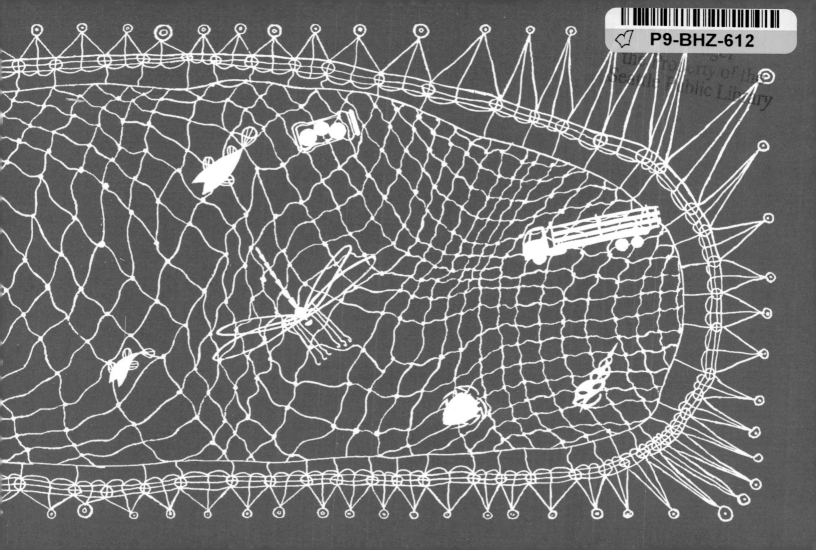

elsewhere
editions

ELSEWHERE EDITIONS, AN IMPRINT OF ARCHIPELAGO BOOKS, IS DEVOTED
TO TRANSLATING LUMINOUS WORKS OF CHILDREN'S LITERATURE
FROM AROUND THE WORLD.

WWW.ELSEWHEREEDITIONS.ORG

João by a Thread

João by a Thread

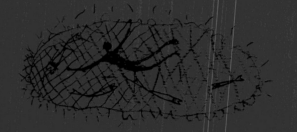

By Roger Mello

Translated by Daniel Hahn

For the children on the Islands
of Uros, on Lake Titicaca

Before he falls asleep, the boy pulls up his blanket:

"So it's just me now," he thinks, "alone with myself?"

How big is the blanket
that's covering João?

As big as the bed?

Or as big as the nighttime?

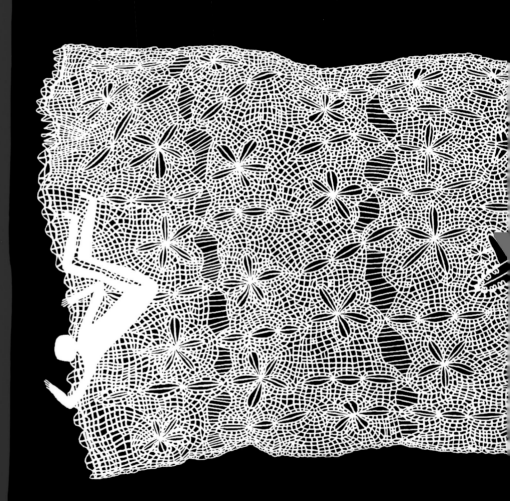

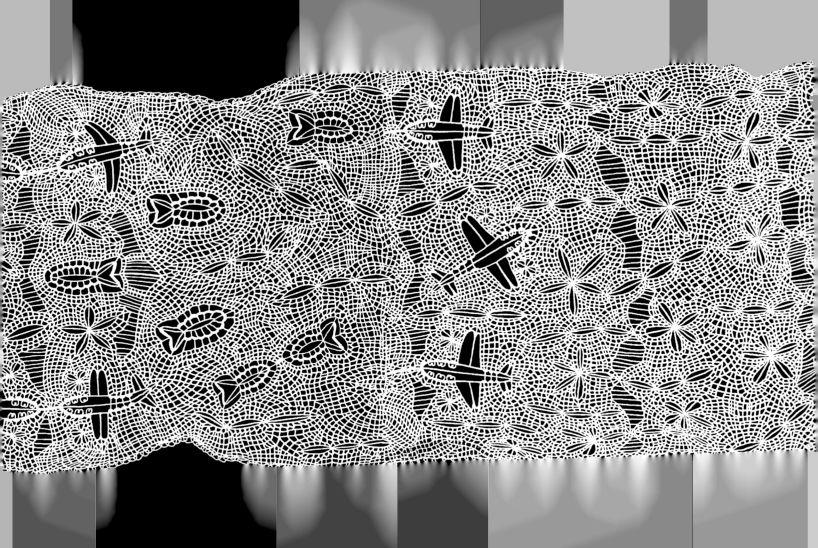

A GOODNIGHT KISS ON THE FOREHEAD NEVER STOPS KISSING.

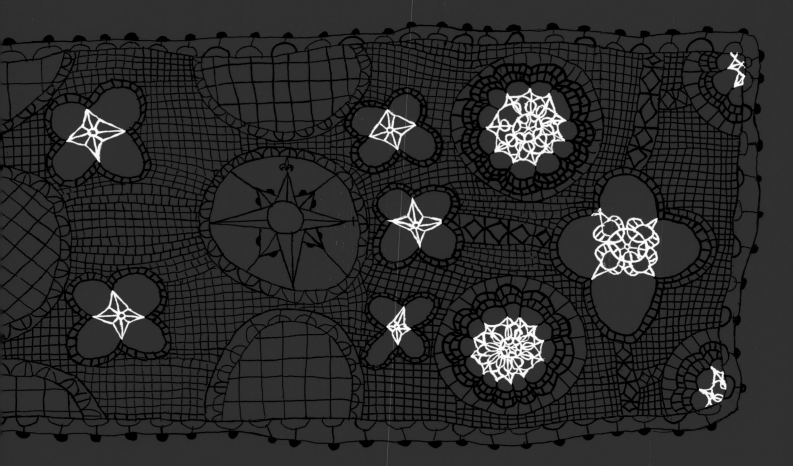

WHERE'S IT HIDING, THE NIGHT THAT KISSES JOÃO?

IN THE STRANDS
OF A LULLABY?

FLUTTERING IN THE WIND?

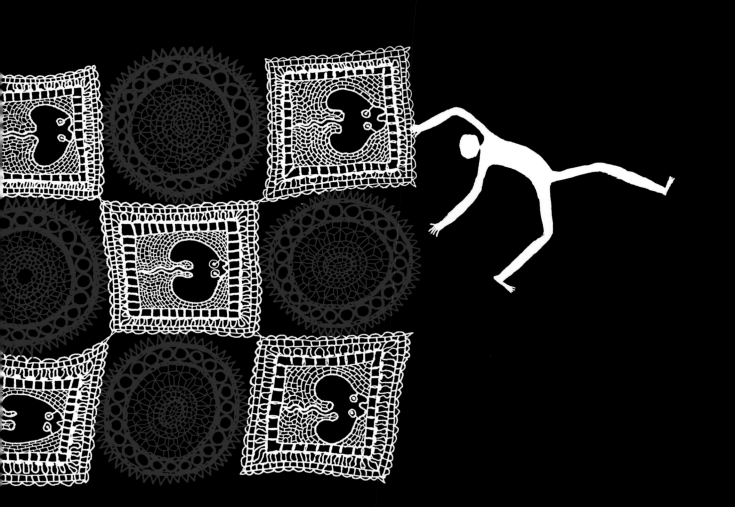

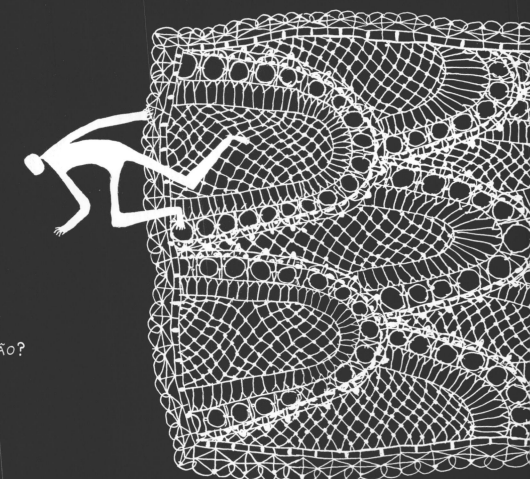

Or in the mountain range
of threads that cover João?

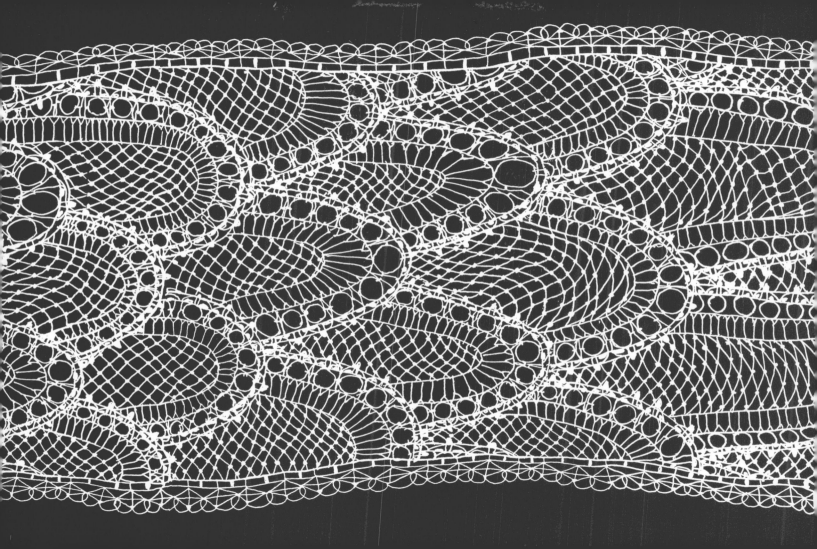

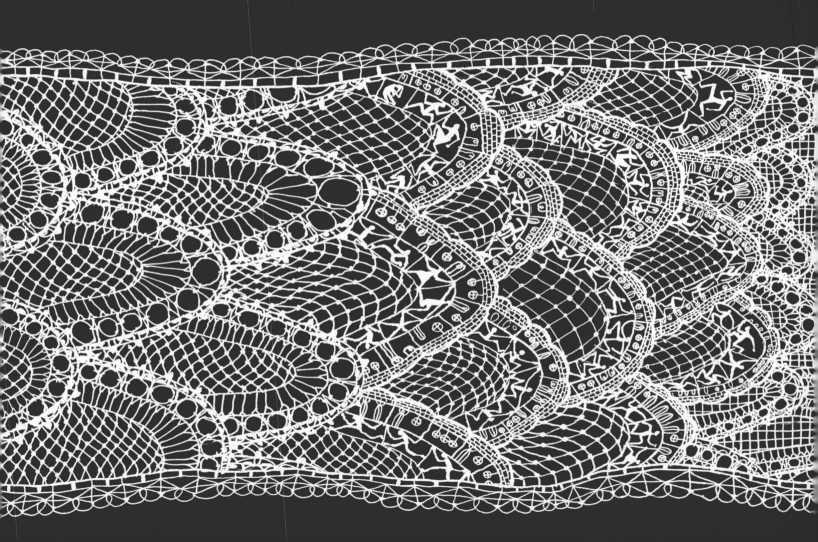

Feet play their game, making earthquakes
under the blanket.
Mountains swap places with valleys.
Meanwhile, little cloth cities
try to predict the next tremors.
Who's afraid of a giant called João?

WHEN IS THE GIANT GOING TO SLEEP?

MAYBE WHEN HIS FATHER GOES OUT FISHING?

If João does fall asleep, what landscapes
does he dream about?
Soft rivers? Bedsheets of water? Lakes? Reservoirs?
Dreams soaked in fear?
And if the fear spills over,
is it João who's turning on the faucet?

JOÃO LETS A LAKE
OF FEAR POUR OUT,
OVER TADPOLES AND SEASHELLS.
A CIRCULAR LAKE,
FLOODING THE BLANKET.
FISH MORE SLIPPERY THAN SOAP.
WHAT NET COULD EVER HOLD
A FISH THAT'S BIGGER THAN US?

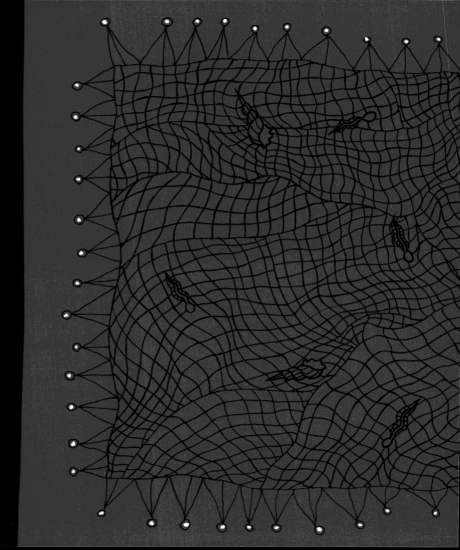

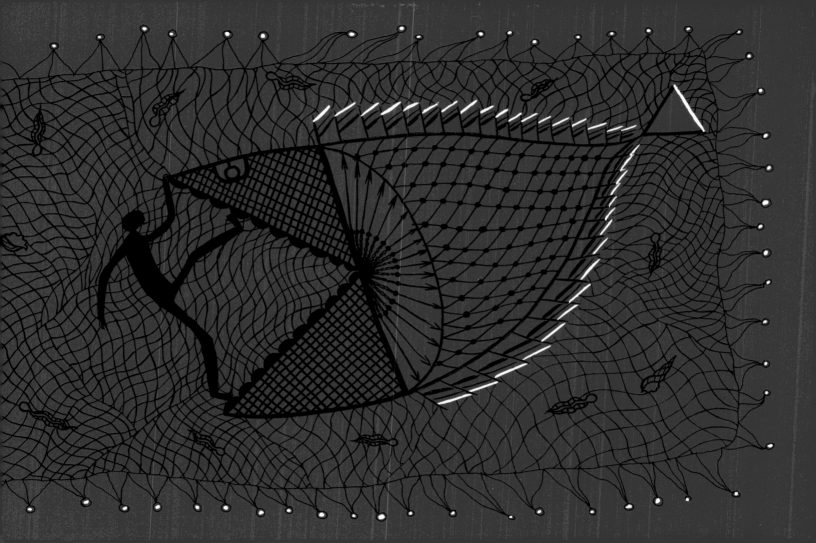

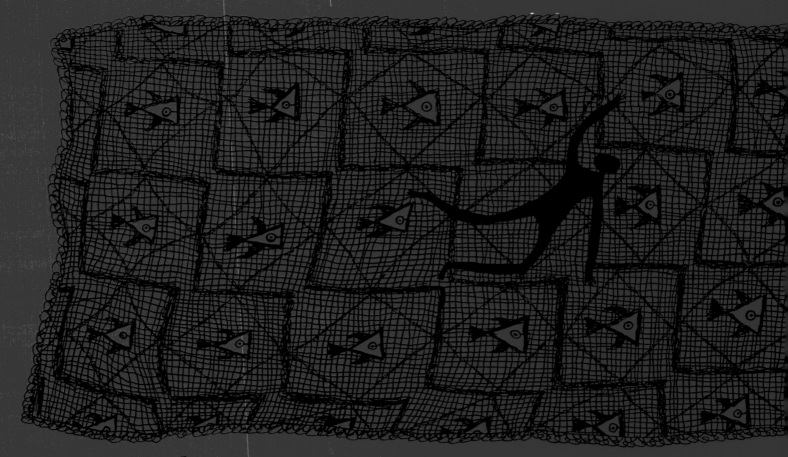

THE FISH BREAKS THROUGH THE WEAVE OF THE NET.

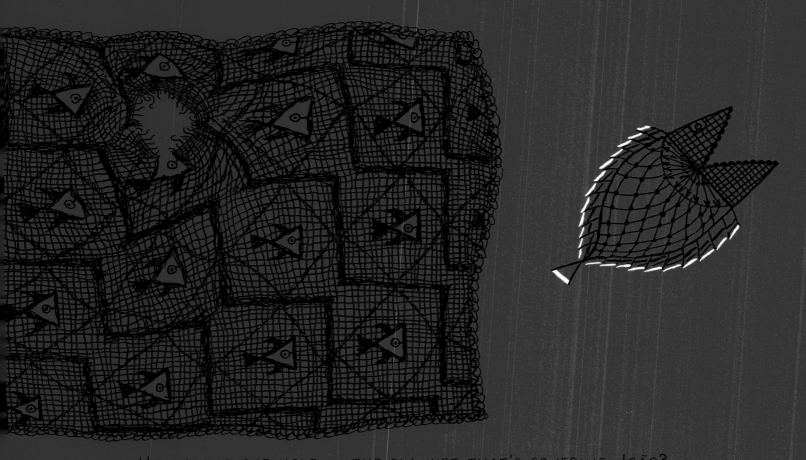

How big is the hole in the blanket that's covering João?

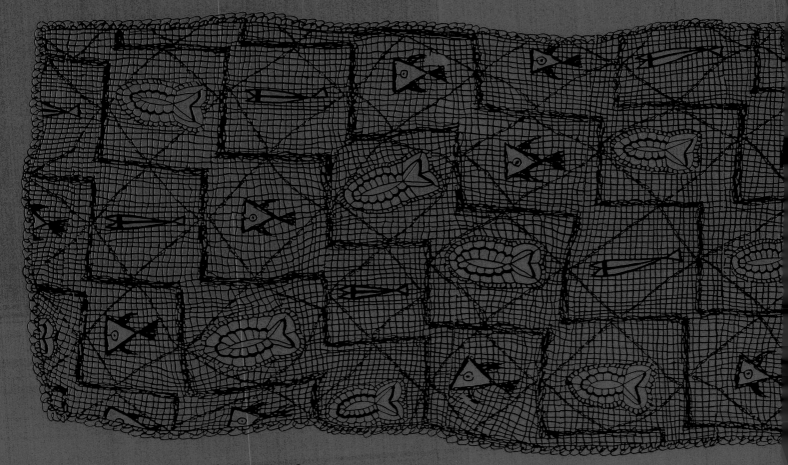

ONE PALM? TWO PALMS? THREE METERS?

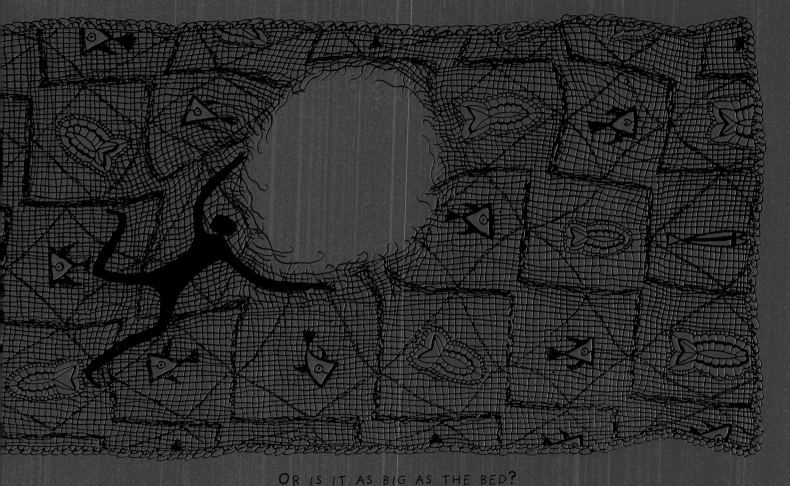

OR IS IT AS BIG AS THE BED?

A HOLE THAT SWALLOWS UP EVERYTHING —

EMBROIDERY, BUTTONHOLES, MOUNTAIN RANGES, SAILBOATS.

HOW DO YOU STOP A HOLE THAT DOESN'T STOP?

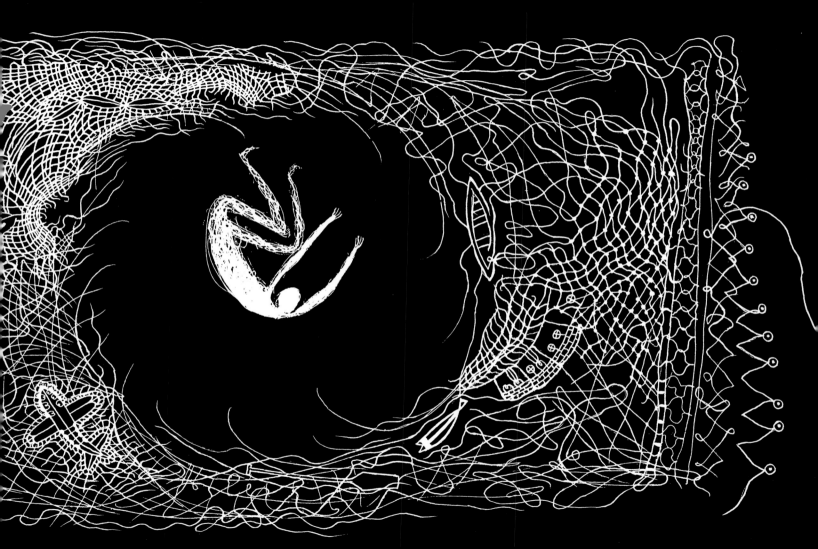

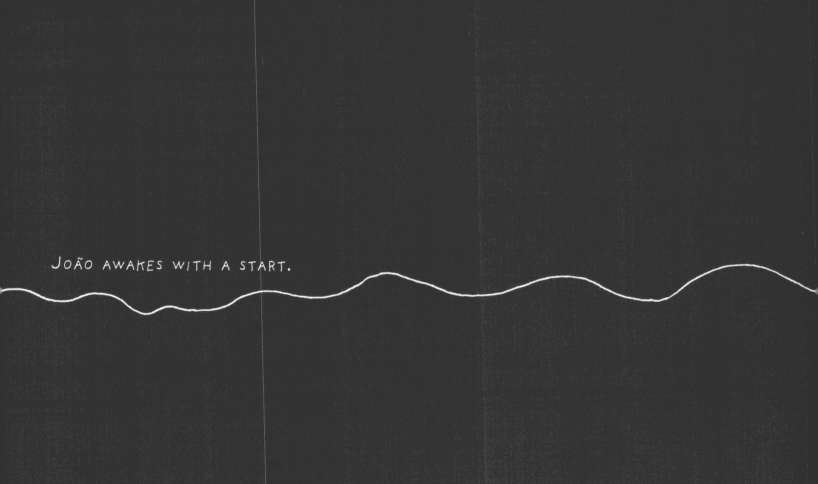

JOÃO AWAKES WITH A START.

How big is the emptiness where João's blanket used to be?

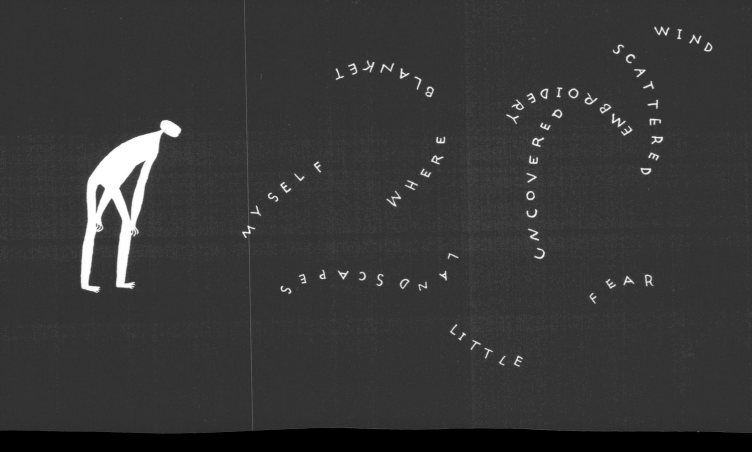

WIND

SCATTERED

EMBROIDERY

BLANKET

UNCOVERED

MYSELF

WHERE

FEAR

LANDSCAPES

LITTLE

A WAKEFUL JOÃO CAN'T GET TO SLEEP IF HE'S UNCOVERED.

IN THE MIDDLE OF THE EMPTINESS, HE SEES WORDS SCATTERED ACROSS THE FLOOR.

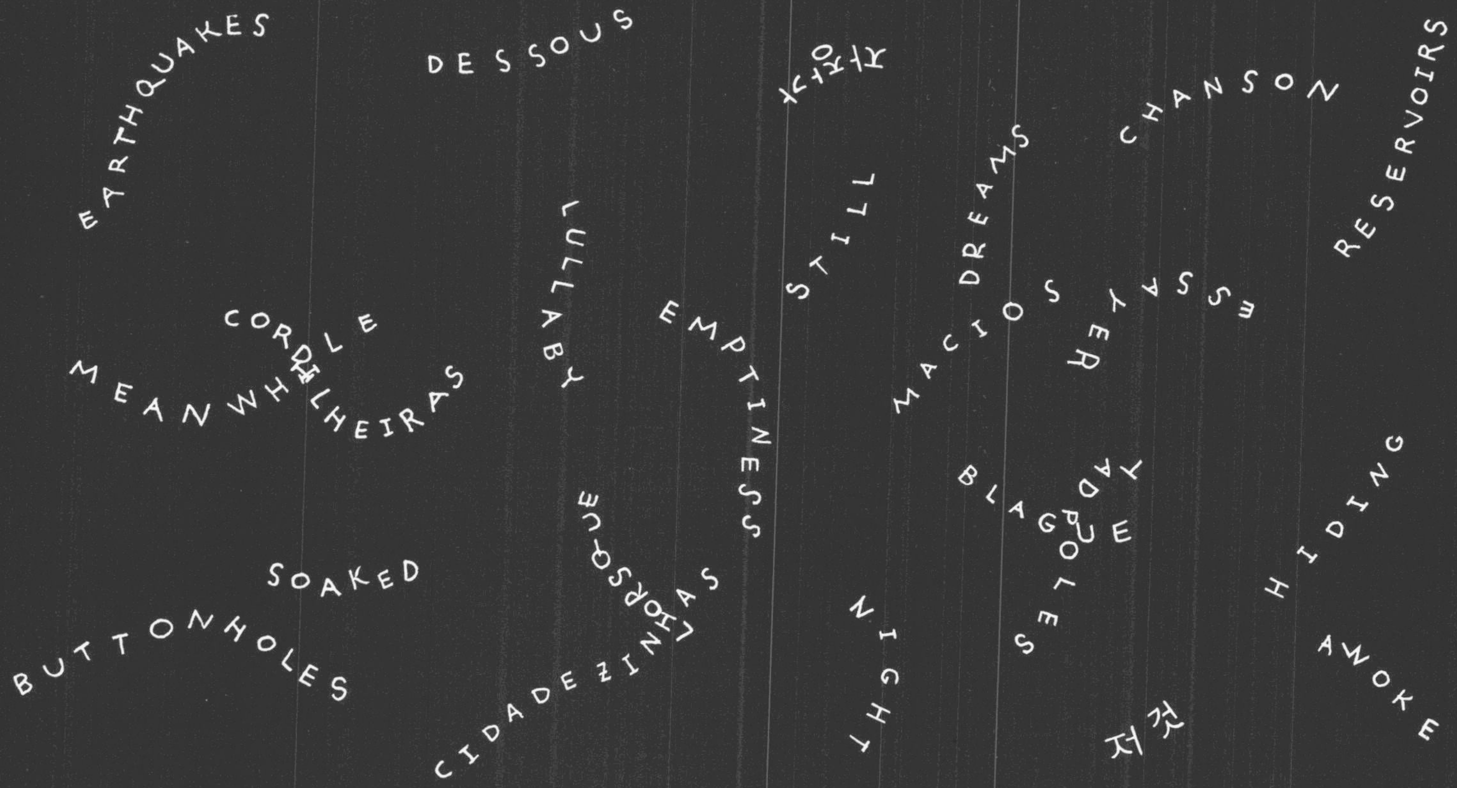

EARTHQUAKES

DESSOUS

천사

CHANSON

RESERVOIRS

STILL

MACIOS DREAMS

ESSAY

LULLABY

CORDILHEIRAS

MEANWHILE

EMPTINESS

SOAKED

LHORSQUE

CIDADEZINHAS

BUTTONHOLES

BLAGOLES

TADPOLES

HIDING

NIGHT

AWOKE

저것

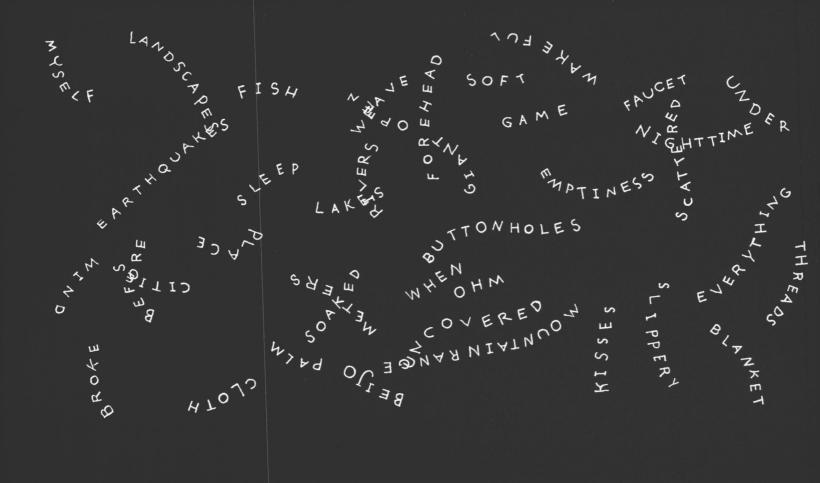

BROKE

START

MATTRESS

TADPOLE

SERÁ

NET

THREAD

THROUGH

OF EMBROIDERS

BED

SPILLING

CLOTH PLACE MOUNTAINS MOUTH SWALLOWING

CHANGE

COVERED FEET

PALMS BIG

HE SEWS THE WORDS LIKE PATCHWORK INTO A BLANKET.
FOR WANT OF A NEEDLE, WILL A QUESTION MARK DO?

As he sews, João makes up a lullaby.

How big is the word-blanket that's covering João?

I was born in London, a long time ago, and it's still the city where I feel most at home. I loved books as a kid, and that part of me hasn't changed one bit either. Actually, I still love kids' books most of all, even now, at my age — is that weird? My favorites were beautiful books in strange colors and surprising perspectives, impossible stories that always made you look at the world a little differently — now that I think about it, I wish I'd had Roger Mello's books when I was your age! Still, getting to work on them now is pretty good, too... (I love them all, but João by a Thread is my favorite. Don't tell anyone.)

—Daniel Hahn

I grew up amid the Brazilian Savanna, in a modern city designed by artists and educators, under an authoritarian regime. While the TV and radio played music and football, the people were searching for their missing relatives — I soon realized what a powerful object the book was, that people could be arrested just for owning them. So I decided to make my own blanket of scattered letters. From animal tales to contemporary arts, I pulled on the thread that connects today's books to an ancient tradition. Just like the first piece of fabric that sheltered a sleeping child on Lake Titicaca.

—Roger Mello

Elsewhere Editions
232 3rd Street #A111
Brooklyn, NY 11215
www.elsewhereeditions.org

Distributed by Penguin Random House
www.penguinrandomhouse.com

This work is made possible by the New York State Council on the Arts with
the support of the Office of the Governor and the New York State Legislature.
Funding for the publication of this book was provided by a grant from the Carl Lesnor Family Foundation.
Obra publicada com o apoio da Fundação Biblioteca Nacional | Ministério do Turismo.
This book was published with support from the Fundação Biblioteca Nacional and the Ministry of Tourism.

This publication was made possible with support from Lannan Foundation,
the National Endowment for the Arts, the Nimick Forbesway Foundation, and the New York City
Department of Cultural Affairs.

Printed in China

This book was set in Providence Sans. The images were scanned by Celso Cury.
Typesetting by Zoe Guttenplan